Ladybird

This Little Story

belongs to

Published by Ladybird Books Ltd
27 Wrights Lane London W8 5TZ
A Penguin Company
3 5 7 9 10 8 6 4 2

Printed in Italy

Bold
Little
Tiger

by Joan Stimson
illustrated by Jan Lewis

Each morning, when he woke up, Little Tiger always said the same thing:

*"I'm tall and I'm tough.
I'm growly and gruff."*

And then he prowled proudly round his Big Sisters on tiptoe.

Good morning, Big Sisters!

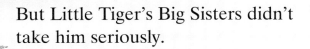

But Little Tiger's Big Sisters didn't take him seriously.

"You're not grown-up enough to come with us," they told him.

So one day, Little Tiger set off on an adventure… all on his own.

Not far from home was a steep bank.

"WHEEEEEE!" Little Tiger was just whizzing down it for the tenth time, when he heard a cry for help.

Instantly, Little Tiger was on the alert.

Wheee

Watch your paws, Little Tiger!

"I'm tall and I'm tough.
I'm growly and gruff,"
he called. Then he picked himself
up and leapt off to investigate.

A little way down the track a mother tiger was wailing and pointing to a rocky ridge.

"My cubs are stranded," she groaned. "I only turned my back for two minutes and they crept off... along that narrow ledge."

"*I'm* too big to reach them," explained Mother Tiger. "And they're too frightened to crawl back by themselves."

Little Tiger drew himself up to his full height and looked bold.

"I'm tall and I'm tough.
I'm growly and gruff…"

he told Mother Tiger. "And I'm exactly the right size to rescue your cubs."

We didn't mean to come this far!

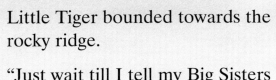

Little Tiger bounded towards the
rocky ridge.

"Just wait till I tell my Big Sisters
about *this*," he thought to himself.

Before long, he was able to leap
onto the narrow ledge where the
cubs were huddled together.

"I'm tall and I'm tough.
I'm growly and gruff…"
bellowed Little Tiger, "And here
I am to make one of my daring
high ridge rescues."

Little Tiger waited for the cubs to tell him how brave he was. But to his horror, they scuttled backwards… towards the edge of the ridge.

"Don't shout!" they whimpered. "We're scared and we want our mum."

"Oh, no," groaned Little Tiger. "These cubs are so frightened that I'm going to have to WHISPER. And I haven't done that since I was a cub myself."

Little Tiger looked nervously over his shoulder.

"Thank goodness my Big Sisters can't hear me," he told himself.

And at last he managed a whispery hiss.

"I'm a friend," he explained to the cubs. "And I've come to help you."

To Little Tiger's relief, the cubs stopped scuttling backwards. But then they refused to climb onto his back.

"We want a story first," they announced. "Mum always tells us a story when we've had a shock."

Oh, no!

"A STORY!" bellowed Little Tiger.

*"I'm tall and I'm tough.
I'm growly and gruff…*
and I didn't crawl along this
dangerous ledge to tell stories!"

But when the cubs leapt backwards
again, Little Tiger was forced to
think quickly. Once more he looked
nervously over his shoulder.
"At least my Big Sisters can't see
me," said Little Tiger.

Don't be frightene
of him.

And then he began, "Once upon a time there were two tiny tigers…"

"Oooh!" squealed the cubs, "that sounds exciting." And they listened eagerly as Little Tiger told the tale of two small cubs who had to be rescued… by the bravest and boldest tiger in the jungle.

At last the cubs clambered onto Little Tiger's back.

They're happy now!

"Hold tight," he told them. "And look straight ahead to where your mum is waiting."

At the word 'mum' the cubs began to whimper again.

"We want our mum," they sniffed. "We want her to hug us and to sing *The Little Jungle Jingle*." But then they had a bright idea.

"You can sing *The Little Jungle Jingle* with us," they told Little Tiger. "And then we won't be frightened."

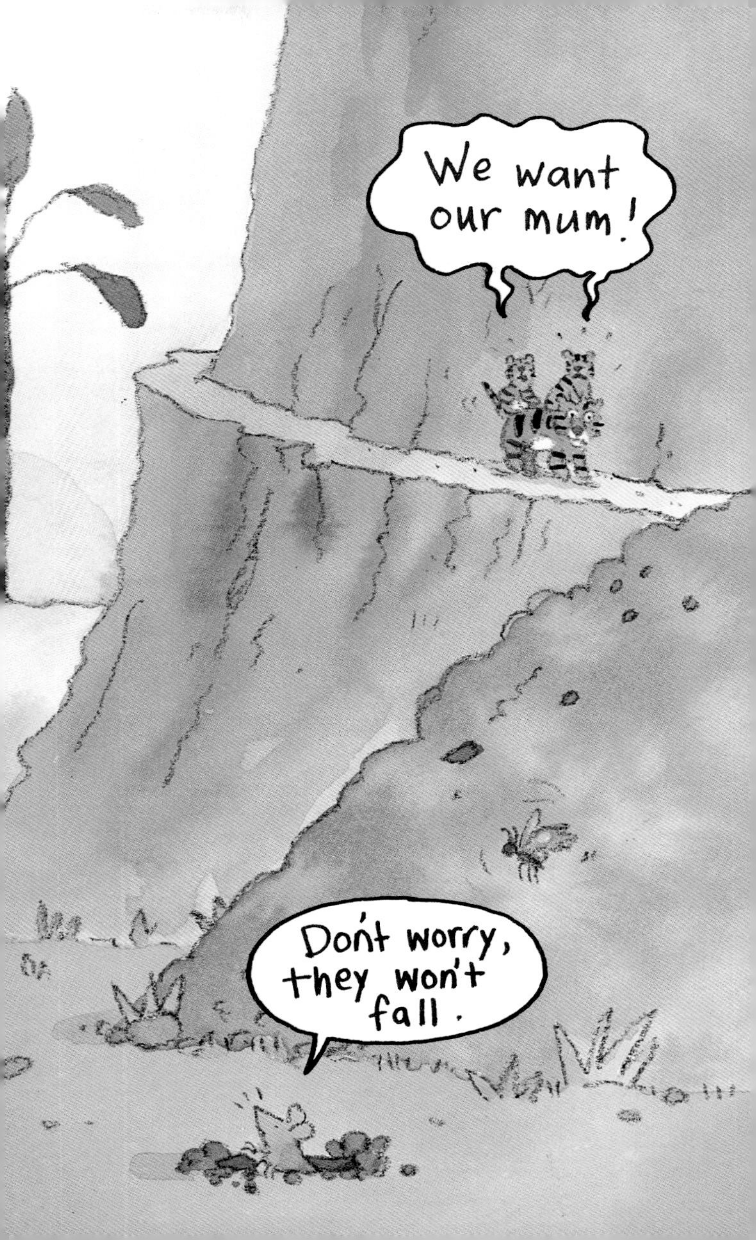
We want our mum!
Don't worry, they won't fall.

Little Tiger nearly fell off the narrow ledge.

"THE LITTLE JUNGLE JINGLE!" he hissed. "I don't know the words to any Jungle Jingle."

"We do!" chorused the cubs. And as soon as he'd checked that his Big Sisters were still out of sight, Little Tiger was forced to sing…

Jungle cubs, jungle cubs,
Jog along the track.
Fur, paws and BUMPSY cubs!
It's time we all jogged back.

By the time he'd wriggled and sung
his way to the end of the ledge,
Little Tiger was *EXHAUSTED*!

But Mother Tiger was beaming with relief. And Little Tiger's Big Sisters had arrived to see what all the noise was about.

"Listen to us," shrieked the cubs. "And listen to Little Tiger join in."

"OH, NO!" shuddered Little Tiger. "I'm going to have to sing *The Little Jungle Jingle* again. And this time my Big Sisters will hear me."

But Little Tiger was in for a
surprise. Because, by now, the cubs
were prowling round their mum on
tiptoe and growling,

*"I'm tall and I'm tough.
I'm growly and gruff…*

and, when we grow up," they
announced, "we want to be as
brave and as bold as Little Tiger!"

"Of course you do," said Mother Tiger. "Anyone can see that Little Tiger is a very bold tiger indeed. And I couldn't have managed without him."

Little Tiger's Big Sisters looked at each other in amazement. Then they took a long look at their brother.

"Come on, Little Tiger," they both cried at once. "It's time you joined in with *us*!"

We're tall and we're tough.
We're growly and gruff,
and we all ROAR together!